This is the sun

Or is it?

Mrs. Acosta-Reyes

This is the sun
Or is it?

Written by Kathryn Knight
Illustrated by Brandon Reese with **CRAYOLA®** crayons

LEVEL **PRE 1** READER

Published by Dalmatian Press, LLC, 2011. All rights reserved. Printed in China.
The DALMATIAN PRESS name is a trademark of Dalmatian Publishing Group, Franklin, Tennessee 37067. 1-866-418-2572

CE13176/1110

This is
the sun.

Or is it?

This is
a flower.

Or is it?

This is
a lion!

Or is it?

Is this a dandy lion?

Yes, it is!

(It is a dandelion.)

This is
a pink
worm.

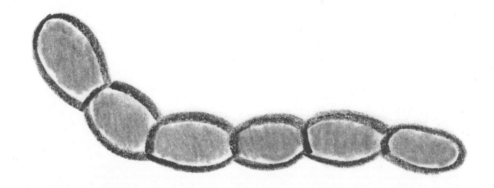

Or is it?

This is
a floppy
hat.

Or is it?

This is
a jelly
fish.

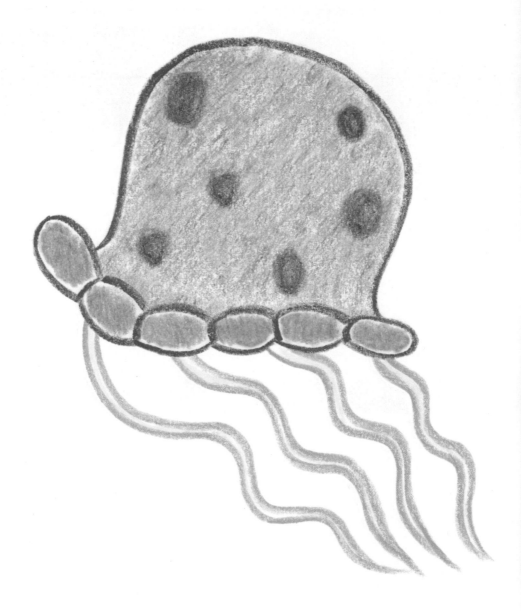

Or is it?

Is this
a snail?

Yes, it is!

This is
a gray
rock.

Or is it?

This is
a spotted
egg.

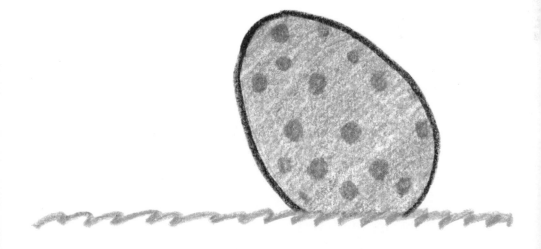

Or is it?

This is a little bug.

Or is it?

No!

This is a **BIG** bug!